PIPE DREAMS ON PICO

Brent L. Smith

Cover Artwork by Olya Dyer

"Street Justice" excerpt re-printed by permission
from Death Valley Girls

www.farwestpress.com

First Edition

ISBN 978-1-7365388-2-1

Printed in the United States of America

For Sandra & Lynette

"You're a creature

Of destruction

I bet you know

Into the night

Into the night to fight

Come on, baby

Let's fight"

45 GRAVE, "Evil"

The Driver inches the black '99 Mustang SVT Cobra along a jammed Pico Boulevard with the top down. Exhaust fumes from the endless line of cars distort the palm trees and blue sky in the side view mirror. She checks her pale lips sliding her tongue along the front of her crooked pearly whites and shakes her wild, curly, burning red hair to "Drive Your Car" by L.A. Witch playing on local radio through heavy static. Black wraparounds hide her yellow eyes.

She reaches into her black leather thrift store purse between the seats and out slides a pipe bomb. With bony fingers she lovingly caresses the outer shell—duct-taped with rusted nails and broken glass. The bomb's improvised machinery chockfull of burning potential.

The Passenger takes it from her. Then out slides another. Then another. With her red eyes and long, straight yellow hair, the Passenger locks an ecstatic gaze with the Driver. She then passes the bombs to the Backseat Third—orange eyes, yellow brows, shaved orange hair, and neon orange lipstick.

They Three speak without speaking. Telepathic kindred. The circle is complete. They may not know how they were born, but they know why they were born.

The Driver veers a sharp left onto San Vicente

and then a sharp right onto Venice Boulevard, pulling into the parking lot of the Bank of America lousy with customers on a late Friday afternoon. The sinking sun kisses the horizon. Shadows long in burnt gold dark light.

The Driver backs up with the rear of the Cobra facing the double entrance doors, smiling at weirded-out folk as they exit the bank. The Backseat Third lights the fuses of each pipe bomb. With the gear in reverse, the Driver steps on the pedal and the Cobra crashes straight through the doors. Glass shatters and people go diving and screaming every which way. The Backseat Third chucks the bombs in.

One…two…three.

The Driver drops into first gear and tears outta there in a loud screech. They hear behind them the loud, concussive blows.

One…two…three.

Screams and busted glass and car alarms ring throughout the busy intersection.

The Driver's face splits into an awful smile. The Passenger turns around to face the scene. Her eyes light up like hell—a sparked Bic inside her skull.

The motorized top of the convertible goes up, covering They Three like a shell, and the Cobra disappears into the mass of automobiles littering the endless boulevard.

Oil and Banking Giants Spend Millions Lobbying to Block Climate Change Policies read the headlines in rows of busted newspaper vending machines long abandoned along Pico Boulevard.

Detective Stokes speeds past, kicking up trash in the night air. The blue flashing siren light illuminates the interior of the black, unmarked 2019 Dodge Charger SRT Hellcat.

She arrives at the scene of a burnt-out Bank of America. Survivors huddle in trauma blankets and struggle to answer questions while the dead are zipped up and hauled away in black body bags. She approaches her commanding officer, Captain Mannix, who immediately recognizes her raven hair and black sunglasses that never come off. Next to Mannix is a somber middle-aged man dressed like a door-to-door salesman.

"Stokes, this is Larry Orr, arson and bomb investigator," Captain Mannix says, introducing them. "Larry, this is Detective Mel Stokes."

Stokes gives Orr a dismissive handshake, then back to her Captain, "What are we looking at?"

"Witnesses report three separate explosions. Looks like improvised devices."

"Anyone get a look?"

"A vehicle reportedly backed in through the front entrance. The explosives were thrown from the vehicle before it took off."

"How many perps?"

"Three."

"No one got out of the car and entered the building?"

"Nope. Robbery was first called on, but no money was stolen, so they're handing this off to you."

"Camera footage?"

Orr and Captain Mannix glance at each other uncomfortably. Stokes is handed a tablet.

"We got this from the branch manager…"

When Stokes hits play the grainy footage shows everything in the bank normally. But once the Mustang plows through the doors, the image of the car and its inhabitants is distorted.

"What is it?" she asks.

"We don't know," Orr tells her. "Maybe it's the camera, or some unidentifiable heat signature. Strange, is all."

"Point is, we can't get an I.D.," Captain Mannix tells her.

"So, no APB?" Stokes asks.

"On what?" Mannix snorts. "An optical illusion?"

"Three men in a convertible should be a start—"

Stokes spits.

Orr corrects her, "Women. Eyewitness pegged 'em for women."

Stokes glares at Orr, "Three women in a convertible. We should alert CHP along the 5 and 15, just in case these pyros are heading south. Tell our people no one talks to the media."

"Gotta be just a random act of violence, right?" Mannix shakes his head in dismay. "Goddamn news is already using the word 'terrorism.'"

"The news can say whatever they'd like. They're good at that."

Stokes replays again and again the security camera feed on the tablet. After several minutes, she hands it back with a deadpan calm, "This wasn't random. If this wasn't their first, it's not going to be their last. Feels too specific."

Mannix is relieved she already has a feel for it. "Stokes, I want you to work with Larry here going forward. He's been a consultant for the department a few years now."

Orr is a funny little man, shorter than Stokes and nearly twice as wide. He's sweating through his white, short-sleeved button-up. Even at night. He wears the summer heat 24/7 like a damp towel. Stokes doesn't ever seem to sweat, no matter how much black she's wearing. And she wears lots, head to toe, from black boots to black denim, to a black button-up under a black leather jacket. More mortician than cop.

Stokes eyes Orr like an insect through her black sunglasses and says nothing, just lights a cigarette.

At the Chevron station on Pico and 14th, the Driver stares blankly across the street at Woodlawn Cemetery. Old gravestone silhouettes in the night. It's late and no other cars are at the pumps as she fills up several gas cans lined up on the ground one after the other.

The lone attendant barges out of the Food Mart, "Hey! You're not allowed to do that! Get the hell outta here!"

The Passenger springs from the convertible. The attendant jumps back with prey instinct. She steps under the light where he can better make out her features—rail thin and dehydrated-looking. She's husk-like and emaciated with chapped lips. She rips off her black sunglasses. As if her red pupils weren't odd enough, her eyes then morph to total black and gleam like a serpent under some spell of indecipherable hunger. His astonishment turns to terror. She steps closer. He runs back into the Food Mart and locks the double doors behind him. The Passenger continues to smile, her eyes returning to red. She spins back around and the Driver meets her gaze with a smile. They let out a cackle. Real shrill. Like a preternatural yip. The Passenger hops back into the Cobra, sits on top of the headrest, and points with a long, bony finger at the attendant. The hairs raise on the back of his neck from behind the dirty glass.

The   Backseat   Third   just   watches—silent, withdrawn.

———————

Laughter permeates the midnight darkness of a vacant Venice Beach as a Mustang Cobra burns on the sand. Flames lick the black sky and illuminate the three dark figures dancing naked under moonlight to the soundtrack of crashing waves.

———————

Fast forward. High noon.

A wet rag hanging from the pocket of a car wash attendant is a beautiful thing, like a dead cat lying limp in the mouth of a coyote.

From across the street, the Driver watches through black sunglasses as a blue Ferrari 488 Spider is finishing getting its wax job at Crown Car Wash on the corner of Pico and Beverly Glen. Its owner, a grey-haired suit, is off to the side scrolling through his phone, never looking up at the detail. He's in white linen pants and a pinstriped collared shirt unbuttoned at the top, exposing chest hair. His clothes say Casual Friday every day of the week but his life is all business and never ending.

They Three coolly sit in a maroon 1969 Mercury Cougar, parked in the red in front of the tranquil and ancient façade of St. Timothy Catholic Church.

A song on local radio ends in distorted guitar rambling and banging cymbals. The stoner DJ speaks, "That was 'Zombie' by the Coathangers. Before that was the Cramps with 'Don't Eat Stuff Off The Sidewalk' from *Psychedelic Jungle*. Sage advice, if you ask me. We got some Starcrawler crawlin' at ya here on Gidget's Garage Rock Jams. Stick with us, we're spinning this wax all weekend here on KXLA."

The church doors open and out floods crowds of

families in funeral clothes down the steps.

The suit hands the sweaty car wash attendant holding his door open only a stub and no tip. Hardly looks up from his phone as he gets in and fires up the Spider and screeches out of the parking lot.

"I Love L.A." by Starcrawler starts playing. The Driver fires up the Cougar—real loud growl—startling the churchgoing families. The Passenger notices a little boy gawking at them in a schoolboy uniform and matching newsboy cap. She slides her sunglasses down her face, smiles wide—unnaturally wide—and sticks out her tongue. He takes one look at her red eyes and ghoulish smile and screams for his mother as the Cougar tears outta there and onto Beverly Glen.

Living ▮▮▮▮▮▮▮
Cruising ▮▮▮▮▮▮▮
▮▮▮▮▮▮▮▮▮ *nightmares.*

They head north toward Olympic, tailing the suit in the Spider as he weaves carelessly through traffic. Palm trees that line the center divider flash by in frames.

They cross Olympic, then Santa Monica, then Wilshire. The suit notices the same maroon muscle car has been following close. He changes lanes, then it changes lanes. He slows down, then it slows down. He speeds up, then it speeds up. The Cougar gains ground on the Spider, inching closer as the Playboy Mansion passes by on the right. The suit glances in the rearview again, startled as he sees three elongated smiles coming from the car behind him. Ear-to-ear like three dirty pearl necklaces. But they don't seem like the pearl necklace types. Not the way they're driving.

The Driver downshifts into second gear and the RPMs redline. They pull up beside the Spider. The nervous suit speeds up as both cars barrel toward the narrow corridors of Sunset Boulevard.

He can hear them laugh as they swerve into his lane, making him maneuver erratically. He floors it and puts the Cougar behind him, reaching 70mph as they dash across Sunset. He makes a sharp left to stay on Beverly Glen. Cross traffic honks and screeches to a halt as the Cougar sticks close behind.

It's now an all-out chase up the winding road, the suit passes cars and weaves desperately through oncoming traffic. Stone Canyon Reservoir glistens over the hills to the left. The Cougar screams up behind him, rubbing his back bumper. The suit hits the steering wheel with his fists in frustration. His luxury sports car should be putting these chicks in the dust. Who are they? What do they want? He punches it into high gear, nearly losing control as the Spider climbs higher. He reaches the crest of Mulholland Drive.

The summertime city is beautiful and clear below.

He skids left across traffic to stay on Beverly Glen. Sweat dripping from his forehead, he glances in the rearview and sees nothing. He swivels his head around just to be sure. He's lost them. Finally. He breathes a sigh of relief and slows down, turns onto No Name Drive. He laughs like a madman as he pulls into the long driveway of his gaudy Mediterranean estate.

Life is fairytale silent on the ledge of the Hollywood Hills acropolis.

———————

Small surf slaps against the Venice shore in the afternoon sun. Heat shimmers over the pavement like midsummer ghosts, casting mirages in the distance among the graffiti ciphers and hobo hallucinations. The usual sunbathers, skaters, boardwalk freaks, and tourists are distracted, all crowded around the scene on the beach. Detective Stokes and fire investigator Larry Orr were called in to the melted remains of a Mustang Cobra matching the description seen yesterday at the Bank of America.

Stokes comes back from the radio in the Charger, "Ran the plates. It was reported stolen a few days ago."

Orr is on one knee, scanning the exterior of the scorched wreckage. "A cloth doused with gasoline was ignited and stuck into the gas tank," he says. He takes photos with a disposable camera.

"How can you tell?" Stokes asks.

"The gas cap cover is still ajar. No trace of accelerants anywhere around the car."

"And when we arrived, neighbors reported what sounded like an explosion."

"Right," Orr says. "One big boom."

Seagulls squawk overhead, wings spread, drifting in the ocean breeze. Patrolmen keep the gawking crowd and news crews at a distance.

"Why do this? Why here?" Stokes asks. "Why not leave town and burn this thing in the desert?"

Orr shrugs, "They must want to stick around for some reason. Make a show of things."

"Maybe they're not finished doing what they're doing," Stokes muses.

She hears dispatch chatter from the Charger and trudges across the hot sand. She picks up the mic on the mobile, "Go ahead." After a minute of listening, "Orr! Get in. We got eyes on three strange women in a convertible late last night at a gas station."

———————

Overlooking the twin spires of Century City, the grey-haired suit walks along the edge of the pool in his backyard where his two sons horseplay on a floating chaise lounge in between games of Marco Polo. He enters the home through the open sliding glass doors.

With violin in hand, his wife and a dozen other string musicians sit in a circle in the middle of the massive sunken parlor rehearsing Krzysztof Penderecki's "Threnody for the Victims of Hiroshima." The ominous shriek of strings adds to his anxiety.

No one notices him as he walks by, taking off his sunglasses, his face pouring sweat. He tries forgetting about the last fifteen minutes—the awful nightmare in the stalking muscle car. Hollywood freaks. It didn't happen.

The suit reaches his office—his sanctuary—and closes the double doors and shuts out the eerie string music and his horseplaying sons and the perfect view of Century City through the sliding glass doors out to the pool. His office is cool and dark and insulated from the outside. He grabs a handkerchief on his desk and wipes his face and balding head.

He sits down in a brown leather chair and opens a silver laptop to a login screen. Through the portal are rows of long green figures against a black background. Endless commas and zeros. Alien jargon and encoded virus language of acquiring hundreds of miles of pipeline.

He stops scrolling. The noise of his wife's strings and his sons' horseplay has ceased. The chill of silence. He checks his watch. An hour had elapsed. Missing time. The hairs raise on the back of his neck. Goosebumps roll through his arms and legs. He thinks of his three stalkers. Stop it. Hollywood weirdos. Nothing more. He gets up from his chair and moves slowly toward the door. He puts his ear against it. Hears nothing still. But can feel—heat.

He cracks open the door, peeking out through a sliver. He gasps at the narrow sight of the pool lit on fire—the burning bodies of little boys float on its surface. Before he can process what he's seeing, the office doors fling open, smacking him in the head and he falls to the floor. His wife bursts in, screaming, her body ablaze as it slams violently against the antique bookcase. Fire spreads throughout the room and crawls along the walls. The body crumples to the floor.

The suit scrambles out into the sunken parlor and finds the rest of his home engulfed in flames. He uses his hands to shield his face from the heat. Scattered bodies of string musicians lifeless and burning. In the center stand his three stalkers holding gas cans, stone-faced, unfazed by the fire, eyes locked on him. He stumbles away—tripping over the burning bodies of string musicians—and toward the front door, coughing his guts out, looking over his shoulder at the three figures standing statuesque amidst fire. He twists the knob, opens the door, and turns to flee outside but the Passenger appears suddenly in front of him. He stops in his tracks. She shoves him back into the house. He makes a run for the backyard but runs into the Driver, knocking him to the floor.

The Backseat Third approaches from behind and they converge on him in a triangle. He's trapped. They douse him in stolen gasoline.

"What did I do?! What did I do?!" the suit screams in tears and snot, tugging childlike at the leather jacket sleeve of the Driver, eyes crazed with a terror he's had the luxury to avoid his whole life.

The Driver says nothing, just smiles at him with crooked teeth from ear to ear. She grips his jaw with one hand and raises his face to hers. The flames dance around them, closing in. He feels the heat start to burn away his clothes. He screams in agony but can't move. Fire dances in her totally blacked out eyes. The tears streaming down his cheeks get dried up in the heat. She kisses him on the lips, slithering her long tongue down his throat as his body catches fire. The flames climb up his torso and reach his head and she keeps her lips pressed to his until his muffled screams cease and his corpse withers and caves in to a smoky pile on the floor.

———————

$\mathbf{A}$t the Chevron station on Pico and 14th, Stokes and Orr talk to the lone attendant at the counter. His bloodshot eyes pop under the fluorescent lighting and the blasting A/C hides any hint of sweat as he goes on about what he saw when he encountered the "strange people" in the Mustang late last night.

"They handed me cash for the gas, but it's like they didn't know what it was."

"What what was?" Stokes asks.

"The money. One of them just took out a crumpled bunch of bills from her pocket and held it up to me. 10's, 20's, 50's, 100's. So I asked how much she wanted. She just stood there like she didn't understand the question…but she spoke English. I guess."

"You guess?"

"She understood English, and spoke it, but it was broken, or some weird dialect. It was—off."

"Off?"

"Like playing a record at the wrong speed. You know, off."

"What did she look like?"

"Taller than me. Very tall. Maybe 6'2. Maybe taller. Red hair. Like fire. Skin was so pale. Nearly grey. I

23

couldn't see her eyes because of the glasses. But she looked sick. Like, very dehydrated and emaciated. But she was smiling at me. She wouldn't stop. It made me nervous. I don't scare easy. But this wasn't normal. I didn't like it."

"Did you get a look at the others?" Stokes asks.

"No…and yes."

Stokes looks confused.

The attendant goes on, "It wasn't until they started filling up the gas cans that I came out to yell at them. And then one of them jumped out of the car and confronted me—"

He hesitates for a moment, as if questioning what he himself saw.

"She took off her sunglasses. I—saw her eyes." He makes the sign of the holy cross across his chest. "They…" he begins to choke on his words, "it's like… they… weren't human."

"Go on."

"She had red eyes. But that wasn't the worst of it. When she got angry at me for yelling at her friend, her eyes—even the whites of her eyes—turned black."

Stokes takes notice of the small bottle of Jim Beam the attendant has stashed behind the counter.

"I see. Thank you for your time, sir."

"Please make sure they never come back!" the attendant yells as they leave. "Please…PLEASE!"

They ignore him and walk outside.

A hot breeze hits the palm trees in the washed

out sunshine, making them sway over the serene headstones of Woodlawn Cemetery.

Stokes mulls over what she just heard.

"What'dya thinking?" Orr asks.

"I'm thinking this shit's too weird. Even for L.A."

They get into the Charger.

Orr takes a deep breath. He's probably in over his head. He's encountered some screwball pyros in his time, but what's he supposed to make of this? He checks his phone. "Look, the wife's been calling. When do you think I can go home?"

Stokes hears a call from dispatch. She picks up the mic, "Go ahead," and listens to the small electronic voice report a 451 at Mulholland Estates. Her demeanor grows tense, "On our way."

Stokes hangs up and starts up the Charger, RPMs redline. "Orr, you're not going home."

———————

In the Norma Triangle on Santa Monica Boulevard, the Passenger and Backseat Third wander through the aisles of Koontz Hardware Store, scanning the shelves, feeling the displayed tools and supplies like found artifacts. The older and otherwise friendly sales associates avert their gaze, too timid to throw out their usual line, "Can I help you find something?" Instead they bury their heads in merchandise, feigning busyness, sticking price tags on items, pretending they don't see.

The two strange girls approach the checkout stand, each dropping obscene amounts of steel water pipes onto the counter. They do nothing but lock eyes with the nervous checkout clerk, and smile like aliens who have just learned about the human custom of smiling. The clerk says nothing as she quickly scans the barcodes on the pipes. It feels like an eternity. All the air's been sucked from the store. The cashier feels a rush of heat. Sweat beads on her forehead and she feels her shirt stick to the small of her back. She scans the other items—20ft. roll of green fuse normally used for model rocketry, a roll of duct tape, and a box of nails. The Passenger lays down crumpled bills—the edges burnt and caked in ash—takes the bagged items, and doesn't bother with the change as they leave through the double doors and out to the purring idle Cougar where the Driver waits for them.

_____

Stokes parks the Charger and takes long strides up the narrow street of No Name Drive. The commotion of emergency vehicles just up ahead. Orr struggles to keep up with her pace.

"So, no partner, huh?" Orr asks, already short of breath.

Stokes says nothing.

"Did you used to have one? What happened to 'em?"

Stokes remains silent. She doesn't want to think about her old partner, or what happens to the world when it loses the good cop.

"Hey, I get it," Orr says, happy to prattle on. "I'm retired. It's nice not to be tied down. Fought fires for 35 years. Even put in some time as a smokejumper. But, hell, that's a young man's game. Started the firm two years ago just to keep myself busy."

Stokes stops in her tracks, looking down at the street.

"What is it?" Orr asks.

"Skid marks. See these? They look new."

"Oh, yeah. Some hot rod?"

27

"You'd have to be crazy to speed down these streets. Look. Two different tire tracks. They lead up to the house. Somebody was heading here in a hurry."

Orr snaps a photo of the tire tracks with his disposable camera.

Fire crews finish up, spraying what's left of the black rubble and hacking with axes at the rooftop. A young LAPD officer greets Stokes and Orr.

"What do we got?" Stokes asks.

"Fifteen bodies, give or take," the officer responds somberly. "High-profile, too."

"How's that?"

"This is the residence of Robert Z. Pinsmeister."

"Who?"

"Chief Executive Officer for BP. He was also on the shortlist for the president's choice for head of the EPA."

"BP?" Orr asks.

"British Petroleum," the officer responds.

"He ain't British though," Orr says.

"We'll have to wait for the dental records," the officer continues, "but we're pretty sure he and his family are among the dead."

"Yeah, well, first thing's first. Where the hell's the Captain?" Orr lights a cigarette. "And Jesus Christ, get some tape up before these news crews shit all over the scene."

They enter the house.

Orr walks through the scorched parlor, eyeing the debris, Stokes and the officer in tow. Stokes lifts the large sheet covering the charred corpses. "How nice," she says flatly.

They don't look real—more like convincing props from a movie set—until the smell hits. The young officer gags and retches, even though he's already seen them.

Orr is even more composed than Stokes. Not his first rodeo. "I guess this one ain't rocket science," he says, as he kicks a cooked gas can over with his boot.

"Same cans the attendant saw being filled up?" Stokes asks aloud.

"You're the detective," Orr says.

"Bag that," Stokes tells the officer.

Orr takes photos all around with a disposable camera.

The decayed structure resembles Hell suspended in pose. The three of them in the middle of it. What was once familiar is now mutated into bubbled black ruin. A cruel, grand sculpture shaped by a twisted mind, or as if the Earth had reached up and rotted it all from the inside out. Shadows stretch long inside as the day crawls toward twilight.

"Was this where it was started?" Stokes asks.

"No. Point of origin was out by the pool," Orr states, pointing to the backyard.

"That's where they found the bodies of the kids. Sick fucks," the officer says, foaming at the mouth, his youth showing.

"But here's a mass of bodies. So, they came in, dumped fuel all over the parlor, then trailed it out to the pool where kids are playing, and torched the place without any of these people stopping them?"

"Maybe they were armed," says the officer, holding his nose. The stench is potent.

"Then they took off?" Stokes asks aloud.

"No," Orr says, scanning the floor. "Look, there are shoe prints all over. Like biker boots."

"How many you figure?" Stokes asks.

"Two different sets. Maybe three." Orr snaps more photos.

"You're telling me they came back inside the joint while the fire's going?" Stokes asks. "You wouldn't do that."

"Unless something you wanted real bad was still inside."

"But you couldn't do that, right? Physically?"

Orr shrugs, "That's what I'd figure."

Stokes stands silent for a minute. "This feels the same as the bank," she says.

"No explosives were used," Orr points out. "How can you tell?"

"I just know. Any witnesses?" Stokes asks the officer.

"The neighbors. Elderly couple up the hill a ways. They saw a car tear outta here."

Outside in the hectic street crammed with fire

engines, giant hoses, police cruisers, news vans, and milling neighbors, Stokes and Orr question the old couple. They had a more modest mid-century home they've owned for forty years. It was farther up the grade so there was a higher vantage point. The wife wore a permanent expression of terror and disbelief. The husband more stern, taking all this as personally as if it had been his own house.

"My husband was inside," the wife tells them. "I was out watering when I saw three figures walk out of Bob's house. They caught my eye, I've never seen them before. That's when I saw the smoke and realized the whole thing was on fire. They weren't panicked or calling for help or anything. They were just real casual. I thought it was impossible for them to have been in there. To just walk out like that. The flames were already so big."

"They were walking out of the fire?" Stokes asks, confused.

"They walked *through* the fire," the wife says wide-eyed, feeling a little foolish like she was recalling a Bigfoot sighting.

"Then what?"

"Then I called for my husband to come outside."

"They got into an old car," the husband tells them.

"What kind of car?"

"Oh, not exactly sure. Maybe an Oldsmobile. Maybe a Mercury. Haven't seen one of them in years. It was purple, too. Or maybe red. Dark."

"What'd these individuals look like?"

"They looked like punks," the husband barks.

"Y'know, leather jackets and colored hair and shit."

"Who would do something like this?" The wife starts to choke up. "In this neighborhood?"

"Would you be willing to work with a sketch artist?" Stokes asks.

"Of course, officer, anything," the husband says. "I got a real good look at 'em."

"We heard them laughing…" the wife says.

"Laughing?" Orr echoes.

"Snickering. Very high-pitched," the husband says.

"Two of them were skipping. Skipping!" The wife's voice cracks. "Whoever these people are—"

"Punks!" the husband barks.

"Whoever these punks are," the wife corrects herself. "They are pure evil."

The husband shakes his head and the corners of his mouth droop, "Lord help us."

———

Stale twilight sun spills through the old dusty vertical blinds at Ocean Park Pharmacy. The druggist girl sits bored and buzzed and eyes bloodshot on a stool behind the counter, sucking on Northern Lights through her vape pen. A small portable TV sits on top of a shelf behind her, broadcasting local news on mute. On top of that sits an old transistor radio with a broken antennae.

The opening of a Dead Moon song plays from the fuzzy radio on low volume. DJ Gidget mumbles through her dank haze, "Dead Moon has been recently repressed on vinyl. Looks like somebody wised up. Here's one for any L.A. kid who got out of L.A. and is never coming back. The rest of us poor souls are here to burn. Fire season is upon us, kiddies. 'Don't Burn the Fires' here on Gidget's Garage Rock Jams…"

It's a job. An easy job the druggist has (in this quaint little mom and pop pharmacy that's older than she is with faded carpets and dusty greeting cards in rotating racks) while she studies Pharmacology at UCLA on the other side of the 405. She makes no effort to exhale, the smoke spills through her lips as she watches it rise in slow motion like whirling ghosts in the sunlight.

tried
their clothes, *their games*
Being *urban decay.*

In the background of her blurry vision, three beings come into the store, lurching toward her slowly, sharpening into focus through the dissipating smoke. Their thick-soled black boots track dirt and sour green earth across the carpet.

burn *fire*
I'm *home.*

They look like typical Venice leather-headed hipsters in biker jackets and colored hair. Except—they seem different. Not right. Gaunt. Spindly. They're all tall. Very tall. The one in front is a few inches taller than the other two.

"Am—p—heta—mine…" the Driver wobbles.

"What?" slurs the druggist. Eyes glassy and perplexed. She takes in their odor—acrid and smoky. Not like cigarette smoky like forest fire smoky.

"Saaalt—"

"I'm…uh…sorry, I don't understand—"

The Driver pours human riches onto the counter: diamond rings, pearl necklaces, jeweled earrings, cash singed around the edges. The small shiny pile is caked in soot.

"Am—p—heta—mine…saaalt," the Driver's voice carries metallic from her gaunt and pointed face. High cheekbones smudged with soot. She points behind the druggist to the rows of prescription bottles.

The druggist turns, seeing the labels of amphetamine salts. "Ohhh. I see. You need—Adderall? Generic? Okay, look, you can't just buy medicine here. You need a prescription—"

The Driver takes off her black wraparounds. Her

yellow eyes make the druggist gasp. She takes the vape pen out of the druggist's hand and studies it. "Prescript—"

The Passenger walks to the front door and locks it.

The Driver locks eyes with the druggist. "Watch the lights," she orders with a wide smile. Her pupils dilate to complete black and then just as quickly contract into yellow cat eye slits.

"This is really happening…" the druggist whispers.

The Passenger comes back to the counter, grabs a baby blue Bic for sale by the register, takes a few attempts at sparking it and when the flame appears she giggles, like seeing an old friend, and sticks her tongue out and tastes the flame.

The Backseat Third takes the vape pen out of the Driver's hand and holds it in front of her, studying it. After a few seconds it becomes hot in her hand and explodes. POP!

The druggist flinches and covers her face, shielding herself from little bits of shrapnel. When she lowers her hands, they're gone. Had they actually been there? She looks around, spooked. She gets up and walks to the front door. It's still locked. She checks every aisle of the store. She's alone. And when she returns to the counter, she sees the bottles of amphetamine salts are gone too.

On the portable TV, the news reports sketches of the three women wanted by police.

———

"They had this, like, unrealness to them. Or maybe more real than real. Y'know? It was almost kitschy. Y'know? Like, they were outta time," the druggist tells Stokes and Orr an hour later at the pharmacy after they received the call. She's even more stoned than before.

There's a sole patron in the pharmacy browsing old stuffed animals pretending to mind his business.

Poor Orr's face is weary and deflated like an old Bassett hound.

Stokes stands at the counter in front of the druggist with android focus, "Kitschy..."

"Yeah. Y'know? Like old TV monsters ripped right outta the celluloid. Like the Munsters."

Stokes is stoic, "The Munsters..."

"Yeah. Or...well, you know the Cramps?"

Orr lets out a long, deep, frustrated sigh. Deep as the mystery of this lousy fucking case. He walks away and steps outside to call his wife. Gusts of hot winds make the telephone lines pendulate over the loud traffic.

Back in the pharmacy, the druggist goes on, "They stole all the Adderall. And they made my vape pen explode."

"They made your vape pen explode…"

"One of them grabbed it, held it in her hand for a minute. Like, she didn't know what it was, y'know? They were so outta time…" she looks up past the ceiling into the sky talking to no one. She looks back at Stokes, "Then, when it exploded in her hand, that's when they, like, vanished."

"Any idea where they were headed?"

The druggist locks her dark brown eyes with Stokes, "No, you don't understand. I don't mean that they left. I mean that they vanished. Poof. Gone. Smoke."

"Did they say anything else?"

"The one with red hair and yellow eyes told me to 'watch the lights.'"

"'Watch the lights,'" Stokes echoes.

"'Watch the lights,'" the druggist echoes back in a hushed whisper, eyes fixed in a spell.

Stokes takes note of her bloodshot eyes and the empty boxes of cannabis cartridges on the counter near the register. "I see. Thank you for your time, miss."

What nobody knew was that the sole patron in the pharmacy browsing old stuffed animals pretending to mind his business is some journalist who intercepted the call on a police scanner.

––––––––––

Down-and-outers lie in sleeping bags and tents sprawled along the sidewalk in a homeless encampment under the old CLINICA sign on Union and Pico. Across the street, Stokes and Orr pull into Lucy's Drive In.

The bright yellow and white "Drive-Thru" and "Open 24 Hrs" signs shine like beacons in the empty Mid-Wilshire corridor.

Orr gets out and walks to the order window and squints at the menu with pictures of food on it. The eyes of the young brown man at the register keep darting nervously at Stokes, as though he recognizes her. She can see the sweat pooling on his forehead from where she sits. Orr is oblivious, detailing what he would like on his burrito.

In the car, they eat their food in silence. Stokes still has her black shades on. Orr wonders about this, since it's dark out. She wears them like a bulletproof vest.

Chery Glaser comes on the radio with local news. Stokes turns up the volume.

"The manhunt continues for three women who pipe-bombed the Bank of America in Mid-City yesterday. Terrorism has not been ruled out. Eyewitnesses described the peculiar trio as [beat, awkwardly]…'The Munsters.' A 90's model Mustang was found smoldering on Venice Beach, police say there is no connection. More on this bizarre case as we receive updates. Meanwhile, high winds and dry conditions have officials worried about imminent wild fires across the Southland—"

Stokes switches the radio off, "Fucking Munsters on the radio."

Orr snickers into his burrito like a little boy.

"Goddamn snoops," Stokes snarls. "We're keeping off the channels here on out. Just personal lines."

Orr looks at the unit on the dash and snickers some more, "I can't believe you still use a VHF anyway. Why don't you just carry a portable?"

"I like to remain unavailable."

Clearly, Orr thinks. Stokes is tense. He senses it and dutifully straightens up, clears his throat. All business, this one. He takes another bite.

"Alright, so, who the hell are these women?" Orr asks through a full mouth. "Really."

"Not women," Stokes says, before a few beats, doubting her own hunch. She speaks more quietly, "Elementals."

Orr stops chewing, "I don't know what you mean."

"Of course you do. You're a fire investigator."

"I still don't know what you mean."

"Each witness we've interviewed has given us nothing short of—bizarre. Impossible. Paranormal."

"Paranormal? You're seriously keeping statements from some juicer mop jockey and a pothead druggist?"

"What about the statement from the couple on the street? They were straight and genuinely spooked."

"Probably holy rollers," Orr shoos at the air with his hand. "If your neighbor's house is on fire, anyone you see tooling down the street is bound to be the Devil."

"It just doesn't make sense. There's something else about these women. If they even are women."

"What are you getting at?

"I mean...human."

"Are you being serious? You including this in the report? They're just a couple punks with some pipe bombs and a vendetta. What's supernatural about that?"

"There is a vendetta. But what does the bank have to do with Pinsmeister? There was no one to target at the bank, other than the bank itself, and yet Pinsmeister seemed personal."

"It's gotta be some low-rent terrorist cell. Radical commie types. I haven't heard anything serious in L.A. since the 70's. But these eco types, y'know? It never stops."

"There's something else..."

Orr turns the A/C on high. Stokes quickly shuts it off.

"C'mon, Stokes, I'm burning up here."

"I like the heat."

Stokes turns the radio back on and twists the dial. She stops midway through "Earfquake" by Tyler the

Creator.

A dark blue and unmarked sedan pulls into the parking lot and stops next to the Charger. Stokes clocks them for feds but says nothing. The tinted window on the passenger side of the sedan rolls down, revealing two long, pale, bitter faces. They both wear dark sunglasses and short-brimmed fedoras and suits in funeral black. They look like twins birthed from the same rotten, bureaucratic womb.

"What seems to be the problem, officers?" Orr jokes. But his good old boy humor falls on deaf ears. His friendly smile fades.

"You will cease your investigation into this matter," the driver states monotonously.

"Don't you boys have some Russian conspiracies to tend to?" Stokes spits back.

Orr gives a hearty and spiteful laugh.

"Give up your inquiries, and consider this your only warning," the passenger states monotonously.

"We hope, for your own good, that this will be sufficient," the driver states monotonously.

The window rolls back up and the sedan creeps slowly out of the parking lot and vanishes into the black streets.

Pissed, Stokes grabs her cell and dials Captain Mannix. He picks up, already trying to quell her, "Look, Stokes, we knew this was coming. Given the high profile of the last victim. We just gotta take it as it comes."

"I'm not losing this to the feds. Has it even been made official?"

"I don't wanna lose it to the feds, either. I don't know what's happening on their end. I've been briefed and stonewalled all at once."

"I'm not losing this."

"I know. Let's just pretend we didn't have this conversation. Do what you have to do to get this collar, by any means. Quiet and swift. Hear me, Stokes? I mean it. Quiet and swift."

They hang up.

"Everything okay?" Orr asks in vain.

"Yeah. Fuck this. Fuck all of this." Stokes gets out of the car and walks to the order window. The nervous young brown man from before sees her coming and sweats all over again.

"Hello, Freddy. Where's Hector?" she asks.

"Por favor...no sé nada."

"You know who does."

"No se donde esta Héctor."

"Luis would. Where's Luis?"

The young man is hesitant, eyes darting.

Stokes, more threatening, "Where's Luis?"

———

Plan B, the strip club on Pico, glows in a haze of neon in the misty ocean air. The Charger parks in the handicap space in front of the entrance.

"Hate this fucking place," Stokes growls. "A lot of Sheriff's Department on the take. Rarely friendly."

"Didn't this place used to be Tech Noir?" Orr asks, face lighting up like a pinball machine. "Y'know, in the 80's."

"Comin' or stayin'?"

"Oh, I really shouldn't."

Stokes waits, skeptical.

Orr drums his fingers on the door's armrest, "But—I should probably get out of this stuffy car."

They walk through the entrance awning and approach the burly bouncer on a stool at the door. When he asks for I.D. Stokes flashes her badge. The bouncer rolls his eyes. "I wasn't told anyone was coming through. Alright, look, just wait over here and I'll—" Stokes smashes his nose with the teakwood handle of her 9mm Smith & Wesson pistol. She's so quick no one even noticed she went for her gun. The bouncer drops to his knees, reduced to a wailing little boy. Blood out on the asphalt.

Stokes holsters her gun as she walks inside and gives a sharp look at the window girl who doesn't say anything just takes cover charges and doesn't get paid enough to care about who gets their nose smashed.

"Fuck. Shit," Orr says. "Did you have to bust that guy up?"

"Not really. But those feds really pissed me off."

They continue inside through the chandeliers and gilt-framed mirrors and the rest of the forced opulence. A hyper-reality that's more movie set version of a strip club than strip club. "Bark Like a God" by Sloppy Jane plays over the P.A.

Stokes sees her man behind the bar, a handsome cat with a widow's peak and thick mustache pouring a French 75. She approaches, ignoring the two topless dancers fondling each other on top of the bar. The bartender flinches when he sees her.

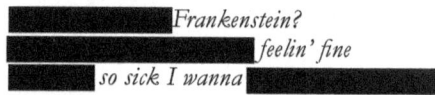
Frankenstein?
feelin' fine
so sick I wanna

"How's it goin', Luis," she says coolly. "I need to find Hector."

Luis is dodgy, "Get you a drink, officer?"

"Don't trouble yourself. I'll get it," Stokes reaches over and grabs a bottle of Old Grand-Dad from the well. She pours two shots and puts one in front of Orr. Orr refuses, and does his best not to pay attention to the dancing skin just a few inches above his head.

"I'm not here to get jerked off, Luis," Stokes takes her shot. "Just be a good boy, and I won't embarrass you in front of your friends."

"I haven't seen Hector since I got out. I don't know where he is. Nobody does. As you can see, I'm on the clock, but maybe you should get in touch with Deputy Rodriguez—"

Stokes grabs Luis's tie, pulls hard, and slams his head down on the bar.

The girls stop dancing and part ways as Stokes pulls out a stiletto switchblade. She pops it open—clean and sharp and four inches long.

"Lie your hand flat on the bar," she orders Luis.

"What the fuck, Stokes," Luis says, grabbing his nose with the metallic taste of blood.

"Luis, I'm not going to ask you again."

Luis puts his hand down on the bar, fingers spread.

Stokes sticks the blade into the bar inches away from his hand. It stands on its own. "You've played five finger fillet, right?"

"Please..." Luis pleads.

"Orr, I'm not drinking alone. Take your shot."

Even though Stokes is about to play a game, Orr realizes she isn't playing around. He looks around and makes sure no one notices while he takes his shot, even though there's no one around who would care.

"Pour us another," she orders.

With his free hand, Luis pours them each another shot of Old Grand-Dad. Stokes takes her shot.

"Orr, take your shot."

"Nah, I'm good."

Stokes takes Orr's shot, then orders, "Alright, hold his hand down."

Orr hesitates, and then grips Luis's wrist real tight.

"Please!" Luis pleads again.

"C'mon, Luis," Stokes whispers. "You wouldn't want your friends to see you playing friendly with a senior detective, would you? I'm doing you a favor. Now you can say you didn't have a choice."

She turns around and meets eyes with the stocky manager standing at the other end of the club with aviator shades on and his arms crossed. He's a spitting image of Richard Berkowitz. The busted-up bouncer stands next to him, holding an ice pack to his face. Stokes provokes them both with a friendly smile and nod.

To break the tension, a one-legged dancer takes the stage and wraps her prosthetic leg around the pole as she executes a twisted ballerina move. She drops her bra. Dollar bills fly and patrons hoot and holler.

gods, _____ and masters
We ____ help
We ____ answer.

Stokes pulls the blade out of the bar, and hovers it over Luis's hand. "Be still now. I've had a few drinks. So, you got a line on Hector?"

Luis shakes his head.

Stokes proceeds to stab at the bar in between Luis's fingers. One. Two. Three. Four. Five. Then back again. Five. Four. Three. Two. One.

Luis gasps in relief.

"Not bad. I bet I can go faster."

"I don't know anything."

"Let's not do this. Is he still downtown?"

"He's off-grid."

"Where?"

Before he can answer, Stokes stabs again, faster this time. One. Two. Three. Four. Five. Then back. Five. Four. Three. Two. One.

She nicks the thumb and Luis spazzes, but Orr holds him in place. Luis whimpers.

"We'll keep it simple, Luis. Tell me where your brother's staying, and I don't tell your parole officer that you skip town twice a month to do your little pick-ups in T.J. Maybe you can even keep a finger or two."

Stokes gets the blade ready for another round.

"Alright! Alright!"

Even Stokes is surprised. She puts away the switchblade. "That was easy. Your own flesh and blood. Didn't you learn anything inside?" she snickers. "Alright, gimme the address and I'll let you get back to work."

Orr lets his wrist go and Luis scribbles on some receipt paper. "I don't have an exact address, but just follow these directions."

Stokes takes the bloody piece of paper and reads it over. Then she slugs him in the jaw. He folds over the bar, groaning.

"That's for snitching. Just looking out for you, Luis."

47

As they exit the club, Stokes tells the manager, "Give the sheriff my best."

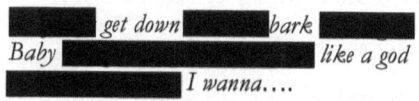

██████ *get down* ██████ *bark* ████████
Baby ████████████████ *like a god*
████████████ *I wanna....*

———————

When they get into the Charger, Stokes seems more calm and collected, even as she rubs her hand still stinging from that punch.

"Everything good?" Orr asks.

"Everything's fine. We're going to Topanga tonight."

"That's all we came here to get? You sure made a mess."

"Just pissin' on the sheriff's turf."

An earthquake rattles the city. They feel the creep-roll of the earth under the car and the back and forth of the palm trees and telephone lines. Car alarms get tripped. It doesn't feel real, like a dream, or a car crash when everything goes in slow motion.

The rattle fades.

Everyone on the street stops and looks around, shock-chatting to each other about what just occurred.

"Jesus Christ. Did you feel that?" Orr asks. "What's happening?"

Stokes starts up the car. "Nothing bad. Maybe a 4-pointer."

Orr gazes out the window and whispers to himself,

"What's happening to us?"

The earth was restless. Stokes could feel it. Something bigger was afoot than a few pyro punks causing trouble. She knew Orr couldn't see past his mechanistic rationality. This was no longer any country for him. Especially where they were headed. He had all the use of an Old West outhouse in an Ursula K. Le Guin novel. Through the swaying palm trees and hazy earthquake weather she saw his future, his nearing fate. She knew she was right, that Orr would never be going home.

———————

Night wind in their hair as they blaze down Pico swerving between lanes around cars the Passenger standing and holding on to the top of the windshield screaming like this was their first day on Earth with a fuzz cruiser hot on their tail, siren wailing. They take a sharp turn down Overland Avenue, barreling toward the Mobile station. Cops see the three assailants bail from the maroon Cougar, their bodies hitting the cracked road and rolling out of sight into the darkness. The Cougar crashes into the gas station and hits a pump. Fireball and sound wave explosion can be felt from the 405. Fuzz tires screech, the cruiser skids, windshield shatters from the blast, cops scream, unable to avoid being engulfed in flame. Disembodied cackling in the night. Cop chopper overhead can't find anything with spotlight in the area that surrounds. Nothing but hot winds and yipping coyotes in the wild brush.

———————

Over the dispatch, reports of a 451 on Overland Avenue. Officers down.

Stokes turns onto Pacific Coast Highway from the 10, heading north toward the Palisades, passing the darkened Jonathan Club and deserted Santa Monica Beach. Midnight.

"That something we maybe wanna check out?" Orr asks. More of a demand than a question. "Sounds like our men. I mean, women. I mean, ghosts…" Orr is feeling a bit salty.

Stokes is enjoying the lip. She wouldn't expect it from Orr. Maybe he's growing on her. Maybe she just likes getting under people's skin.

She flips the mobile unit off. Police chatter cuts out.

Orr jerks, "What're you doing?"

"Radio silent. Off book for the night."

"Why? Who we seeing?"

"Just an old friend. He's usually got an ear to the ground. We'll get some rest for a few hours and head out early. We can check out the scene then."

Orr's irritated, "Yeah…maybe if we're lucky Chery Glaser can tell us what happened."

"I'm sick of being three steps behind, Orr. Aren't you?"

Orr sits indignant and quiet like a shaking dog on its way to the vet. "Three steps behind, three steps in front, what difference does it make? I don't know this road."

Off to the left the ocean shines like black obsidian under the blood moon. The Pacific Ocean, always gorgeous in the sunshine, looks now like it harbors something ugly and sinister below its surface. Demons swim at night.

The black Charger prowls along, camouflaged in all the darkness. PCH is eerily void of other vehicles.

Orr caves to the silence. He senses that Stokes could spend thirty days in the hole and feel at home. But he's the kind of guy that learns a person's life story in line at the checkout stand, and the two of them still haven't had a real conversation.

"So, 'Mel,' is it? Is that for Melanie? Melody?"

Stokes lights up a cigarette, Orr gestures for a cigarette too and joins her.

"Melvin," she answers.

Orr chokes in disbelief, "Melvin?"

"After my father."

"That's not much of a name for a girl."

"It's not much of a name for a man, either."

"How's Pop doin'? He live here in L.A.?"

"He shot himself when I was ten."

Orr wishes he kept quiet, "Oh, I—"

"With the very gun gifted to him by his fellow officers when he resigned from the LAPD."

"Is that the same gun you carry? That fancy little Smith & Wesson you used to bust up that bouncer? Nice piece."

Stokes looks at him but says nothing.

Orr's phone lights up the car's interior. The vibrating buzz cuts the tension. He quickly answers, "Hello? Honey? Can you hear me? No, I'm not smoking. Are you there? I'm not getting good service. Hello?" The call drops. Orr slumps back, closes his eyes and lets out a defeated sigh.

"Nothing gets through these canyons," Stokes says. "What's the deal? Your old lady hard up or what?"

She just wants the topic to stay off her dead father.

"Nah, it's not like that," Orr tells her, looking out the window at the sky. "Eve's great. She's the best."

It irks Stokes to have learned her name.

Orr continues, "To be honest, it's a very stressful time. For years, we tried to have children, and it never happened. We eventually gave up and accepted that it wasn't in the plans for us. That seemed like forever ago. And then, nine months ago, Eve tells me she's pregnant. We didn't know what to think. We were elated, but also nervous. It's what the doc called a geriatric pregnancy."

"You said nine months ago. So, the kid's born?" Stokes asks.

"He's only about eight days old. Eve can't sleep. She's up all night at the hospital worrying. There's something wrong with him. With his lungs. Doc isn't sure he'll make it—" Orr voice cracks.

"She's there," Stokes says. "And you're out here. In the dark. Hunting monsters."

"We can't afford for me to not take jobs," Orr says, guiltily. "The fucked up part is I don't even know my job lately. Thirty years in the field and I just feel dumber. I don't understand fire anymore. The pyro mind. Why this happens. I used to think I did. We think we've got fire down to a science. Truth is, it's as unpredictable as you or me. Car-stealing, Adderall-gobbling punks who stalk oil men and blow up banks? I don't know what I'm doing here."

Stokes says nothing and they sit in silence for a while.

"Don't worry," Stokes says as the car takes a right up Topanga Canyon Boulevard. "This'll all be over soon. One way or another."

They follow the winding road along the creek surrounded by mountains on both sides. Nature feels oppressive to Orr, captured only in the headlights. He can feel it plotting against him in the black beyond.

Somewhere between the Cobblestones and the Purple Stones, Stokes cruises slowly, looking for a small dirt road Luis said would be here. She stops, frustrated, turns around, looks again. Stops, frustrated, turns around.

"We gonna do this all night?" Orr asks.

She looks, and, off to the right, there's a road where there was no road before.

Orr tenses. The tires turn over loose rocks and they go tumbling along the phantom dirt road. Lights from a ramshackle compound appear in the distance. The only lights anywhere in the abyss. Stokes parks in front of the gate and Orr watches as she gets out and approaches a guard on the other side. They talk for a few seconds and he opens the gate. She gets back in the Charger and they pull into the compound. Red taillights illuminating kicked-up dust. Orr watches the guard watching him as they pass. He's holding a Vietnam-era M16 and packs a double barrel sawed-off shotgun in his holster. Orr can tell from his eyes he hates cops, but abides Stokes all the while.

The guard closes the gate behind them. Stokes pulls up to the building and parks. They both get out of the car, silence all around except for the occasional yip of coyotes.

"You can't even tell this is here from the road," Orr says, timid, hand close to his holstered .38 special. "This your friend's place?"

"I don't know whose place," Stokes answers. "Old informant is holed up here. Take it easy, we'll get you some coffee."

Upon closer inspection, Orr gets the impression this compound used to be a small motel, now decrepit and crumbling. A low, flat mid-century style. No, wait, it might be older. Circa 1900. Architectural details come into focus as more exotic with small minarets and scalloped arches. An old monastery? A mosque? What was this place? Silhouettes peek out through curtains in the windows of rooms used for unknown purposes and filled with lights of red and orange and yellow.

An aftershock rumbles through the canyon.

Out of the main building steps a big and burly Mexican with a sour face. He's wearing an old poncho and a bandolier of bullets slung sash-style over his shoulder like a desperado straight out of a spaghetti western.

"Stokes," the big Mexican says, standing tall and threatening. "I told you what would happen if I ever saw you again...."

Stokes curls her upper lip and furrows her brows. Sweat beads on Orr's forehead. He feels for his six-shooter in his holster.

Then the big Mexican smiles and the tension breaks. His eyes reveal a disarming twinkle. Stokes smiles back. Orr is perturbed. They shake hands and share a hearty hug.

"What are you? Some detective? How'd you find me?"

"You know me, Hector. I have my ways."

"Yeah, I bet. Hope you didn't bust my brother's balls too hard."

"Go easy on him," Stokes says. "He cracked before I even got there."

"In that case, fool's dead."

They laugh.

Stokes turns to Orr, "Orr, this is Hector. Hector, this is my associate, Larry Orr. Try not to scare him."

Stokes takes her black shades off. This alarms Orr, as she's never without them. Her eyes are much bigger and brighter and soulful than he had assumed.

They enter the room in the main building. A big, ancient rug is sprawled in the middle, surrounded by cots and aged beanbag chairs and pillows and a few hammocks strung up between posts. Animal skulls hang on the walls and disparate strangers sit in various corners keeping to themselves. The only light comes from candles scattered about like distant stars. There's a makeshift kitchen with a stove and different pots filled with cryptic ingredients boiling on top.

"Tricksters got you chasing your tail?" Hector grins, offering Stokes a hand-rolled cigarette.

Stokes lights up, "So you've been following the news."

"Why else would you be here? No leads, huh?"

"Yeah, I need some—y'know," Stokes' eyes narrow, "—perspective."

"Diableras? Brujas? Maybe they can change into coyotes, disappear, never get killed," Hector continues grinning.

Orr tries to feel less awkward, less out of his element, by getting more businesslike, "Any information concerning the individuals at large would—"

"Take it easy, papi," Hector pats him on the chest. "Take a seat. Get off your feet."

"I fear something far stranger," Stokes continues, exhaling smoke.

Orr sinks down into a beanbag chair with a youthful glee, "Haven't been in one of these since college."

"Fear," Hector says to Stokes, stirring a small pot on the stove. "That's a good place to start."

Silently, with her eyes, Stokes gets Hector's attention. She nods in Orr's direction, as if telepathically, telling him to 'take care' of Orr before they get down to business.

Hector takes the cue, and nods back.

"Here, papi," Hector says to Orr across the room. "We'll get you something hot." He uses a ladle to fill an old dark blue LAPD mug. He walks over to Orr and hands it to him.

"What's this?" Orr asks.

"Tea," Hector says. "We grow our own herbs. It'll help you get some rest. You'll need it for the hunt."

Stokes sits cross-legged on the tattered throw rug in the center of the room. She relaxes her shoulders and body, taking deep breaths. This is the first time Orr's seen her relax anything. He sips his tea happily, relieved to get off his feet and take a breather and not think about nightmare pyromaniacs for a change. The tea is already making him feel lighter, his head tingles.

Hector moves toward the bigger pot on the stove and stirs the concoction, whispering hushed prayers into it. He uses the ladle to fill a wooden cup. He walks over to Stokes who remains cross-legged and still, mentally preparing for what's to come. Hector hands her the cup.

Stokes drinks the tonic. Her body tremors at its bitter taste. She drinks again and nearly chokes. Hard swallows. She drinks again. When it's all gone she falls back into her spine's natural resting place. At first, there is nothing. She sits in lotus, patiently. Hector chant-sings in a bizarre tongue, an archaic yet melodic refrain his father knew and his father before that and so on.

Orr wonders what the hell's going on. But before he has the chance to say anything about it, he feels drugged. His body deadens as he becomes one with the beanbag chair. His limbs are sand. His eyelids are lead. Even if you propped them open with toothpicks, they'd still slice right through. He fights the feeling. He mumbles indecipherably.

After a while, Stokes hears a faint ringing. It comes on louder and louder until it is deafening. A bright, white light with no discernible origin appears overhead and envelopes everything. The room around is torn open like a zipper with the ripping plastic sound of a cosmic shriek. She is now Dream Police. Disembodied everyone everywhere with big remote eye. They are no longer in Topanga Canyon.

Stokes can't control her body, she slumps over on the floor. An old, diminutive Oaxacan woman sits behind Stokes to help prop her up.

"The ones you seek… the ones you seek…" Hector sways, eyes closed, like a palm tree in the firmament. The room is at the heart of the galaxy's supermassive black hole. Spacetime contracts and expands with the rhythm of divine breath. Others in the room come out of their corners. They form a circle and join Hector in primitive drumming.

A bowl is placed beside Stokes whenever waves of nausea hit and she vomits. Her body is like a limp marionette, tops of the strings unseen in the starry expanse above.

Years, centuries, millennia go by. In his hypnagogic state, eyes opening and closing as he fights his paralysis, Orr beholds surreal nightmare machinations in fragments.

The drumming quickens.

On a makeshift altar that has appeared in the center of the room—Hector dissects live frogs—their innards slop down on the altar—their bodies drained of blood into a wooden bowl—on a makeshift altar that has appeared in the center of the room—Hector places a lynx on a table—with a buck knife opens it up—digs in—both hands—pulls out its still-beating heart—slushes it around in a wooden bowl—sits down opposite Stokes—he paints—in blood—lines on her face—chanting spells in a dead language—he paints around her eyes—down her cheeks—a patterned "M" on her forehead—

Stokes is become lynx, knower of secrets. Past and future collapse with present.

The drumming crescendos.

"The ones you seek," Hector whispers to Stokes. "They are daughters of Lilith. Three out of millions. Wrought from the fires within the rifts and fault lines of this old and dirty and evil land."

Orr painfully writhes in the bad wake. He can't breathe in outer space. Behind his eyelids he sees the dark, rolling L.A. hills and bottomless-pit canyons painted in stars. Bad things are coming up out of the crevices to get him, to get Eve, to get his child. He can feel it.

Twin serpents, like holograms, take form and

approach him. Closer. He knows why they're here. They slither back and forth around each other in a figure-eight. Closer. They wrap around him in a caduceus. Their snake eyes meet his. He's seen too much. He's out.

Finally—dreamless sleep.

———————

Sunlight floods the room like a time-lapse video and hits Orr's face. Spacetime resumes its normality.

He awakens and squints in the light. A dark figure cuts the glare and stands over him. He looks up. Stokes looms over him like a dark angel. Her face is clean and clear. Her black hair loose and long and flowing.

"I had the strangest dreams last night," Orr says, harshly. Hair a mess, cheeks stubbly, eyes heavy with black circles. "You see or hear anything weird?"

"No," Stokes answers. She hands him a cup of coffee, crude but hot. Unlike Orr, she gives off an air of rejuvenation.

Orr looks around. All seems well. Sun is out. Sky is blue and cloudless. An old Oaxacan woman sweeps the floor while more coffee brews. Compound dwellers drift in and out helping themselves. None of the prehistoric weirdness and witchy noise of the night before. Of course it had to have been in his head. He thinks. Man. Topanga's got vibes.

"We checking out that gas station?" Orr asks.

"Do you one better. We're headed to Beverly Hills," Stokes says.

"What for?"

"That's where they're hitting next."

Orr furrows his brows, tries focusing his vision. "How do you know?"

Stokes pulls her black hair into a tight ponytail and puts her black shades on. "Call it a hunch."

———

With her crooked pearly whites, the Driver chews on blue tablets of amphetamine salt, looking even more dried out and emaciated than before. Three colorful husks in a black 1969 Plymouth Road Runner 440 Six-Barrel. They stalk two well-seeming gentlemen playing golf at Hillcrest Country Club on Pico and Avenue of the Stars.

"Street Justice" by Death Valley Girls plays on DJ Gidget's Garage Rock Jams. The muscle car prowls a few miles per hour along the curb on the other side of the tall mesh fence that surrounds the course. The men finish putting the 18th hole and get into their golf cart toward the clubhouse.

> *Everywhere we look*
> *Something's burned to the ground*
> *And the people they don't care*
> *Til theirs burns down.*

The Road Runner idles. They Three wait for the men to come out, getting side eyes and glares from country club members walking by. The men come out and get picked up in a 2019 Porsche Macan by their security escort, which includes a chauffeur and a security guard. As they drive off, the Road Runner tails them, slowly and patiently, east along Pico, pushing through the slog of eternal traffic.

> *Nation's head in the sand*

Fingers in their ears
Eyes covered by hands
They don't wanna understand.

The Macan takes a left on S. Beverly Drive and pulls into the entrance of the Beverly Hills Marriott. Stops at the valet. The Road Runner creeps by on the street and they watch the men get out, accompanied by their security guard, while the chauffeur stays in the Macan. They're still dressed in their golf attire: khaki shorts, black belts, bright blue and red polo shirts tucked in. Their pasty skin lightly burned with a piggie pink hue from the morning sun. They head into the lobby.

The Driver guns it and pulls into a nearby alleyway.

Oh, we can be free, we can die in the street
Street justice will prevail
For you and me.

———

Inside the gaudy chic hotel lobby, the men beeline it to the poolside lounge. By the fireplace, a teenage girl in a tie-dye shirt and cutoff denim shorts stands with her handler, a middle-aged woman in an elegant white pantsuit and black designer sunglasses. The girl's natural, delicate beauty is undercut by her look of malnutrition and nervous dread. The two of them look incompatible but people assume it must be a mother and daughter. Upon closer inspection, the girl's eye makeup is running, her purple-dyed hair is greasy and unwashed, and she has bruises on her legs.

The men approach the woman and each shake her hand. Friendly dialogue is exchanged. They don't acknowledge the girl.

The woman says goodbye and leaves the lobby, leaving the girl alone. They both take the girl to the elevator and up to their room. Casual and normal like they're about to have a continental breakfast.

The front desk clerk and other hotel employees glance nervously at the entrance as the Driver, the Passenger, and the Backseat Third enter the lobby. Without speaking, they split up. The Passenger takes the stairwell at the north end, and the Driver and Backseat Third walk across the lobby toward the opposite stairwell at the south end.

On the thirteenth floor, the two men and teenage

girl have already gone into the suite. The security guard sits in a chair outside in the hallway beside the door. He reads the latest issue of *Men's Health* with his wraparound shades on. Sounds of the ice machine being used at the end of the hallway.

He then hears a peculiar sound down the other end of the hall, not the normal steps of just another guest coming and going. He turns to see a sickly-looking girl in the distance, completely nude. It's the Passenger, and her red eyes are locked dead into his. He gawks horridly at her pale, lanky, gaunt figure skulking disjointedly toward him. He's frozen, except for his jaw which slowly drops in shock.

He goes to speak, "Hello? Miss? Do you need some help?"

She doesn't answer. The Passenger gets closer. It can't be real. It's like something out of a horror flick. But he has no time to debate his own eyes. In a panic, he reaches for the Kimber .45 in the holster under his blazer. That's when he feels a presence behind him. When he turns, the Driver swings the bucket full of ice and hits him across the face. Blood and cubes rain all over the carpet and walls. The Passenger and Backseat Third go to town stomping him on the ground. The Driver snatches the .45 from his holster and shatters his skull with three hard blows.

One…two…three.

All is silent in the hallway.

———————

Outside the hotel, Stokes and Orr pull up to the valet in the Charger. When the attendant approaches, Stokes flashes her badge.

"Have you seen anyone strange come in today?" she asks. "Maybe three tall women? Colored hair? Leather jackets? Not very talkative?"

"Actually, yeah," the attendant tells her, wide-eyed. "Really freaked everyone out. We figured they were in some famous band or something."

Stokes and Orr look at each other.

"Keep the car running," Stokes tells the attendant.

She gets out, draws her Smith & Wesson and checks the magazine. She goes to the trunk. Orr follows. She holsters the pistol, opens the trunk, and pulls out a black matte pistol grip shotgun. She loads it. Then she puts on a tactical vest and packs extra slugs.

She stops and looks at Orr, as if to offer him anything.

"You can keep it, Sarah Connor," he tells her. "I'm good with my six-gun."

Stokes is about to close the trunk when Orr stops her. "Actually, wait—you got any cop killers?"

Stokes reaches in and hands him a box of hollow

point bullets.

Orr smirks, "Stokes, you devil."

He loads his .38, spins the chamber, and locks it shut with a flick of the wrist.

Stokes smirks back and slams the trunk closed. They head into the lobby.

Inside the suite's bedroom, one of the men holds a video camera while the other strips the teenager naked, head to toe. He pushes her face down on the bed. He proceeds to tie the girl's wrists together with black rope. He works down to her ankles, ties them together. Then he uses separate rope to connect her hands and feet, hogtie-style. He's done this before. The man with camera, still in full golf attire, conducts an interview. Where did she grow up? When did she lose her virginity? How many guys has she fucked? How many dicks has she sucked? Does anal make her come? She answers each question with blank disaffection, like she's reciting a script. She's done this before.

Three raps at the door. One. Two. Three.

The men freeze, look at each other.

The man stops recording, walks over to the door and looks through the peephole. Empty hallway through fisheye lens.

"Chuck? You out there?"

No answer.

He begins to turn the handle but then stops himself. He latches the door instead and goes back to the bedroom.

Down at the front desk, Stokes and Orr press the clerk about the strange visitors.

"I don't think they were hotel guests," the clerk tells them. "I saw them walk into the stairwell and haven't seen them since."

"You didn't think to call security?" Orr asks.

"They really weren't doing anything—" the clerk is interrupted by a phone call. "Excuse me." He answers the phone, "Yes, I understand, sir. We'll look into it and resolve the issue right away." He hangs up.

"What was that?" Stokes asks.

"One of the guests on the top floor is complaining about noise in the suite next to them."

Without hesitating, Stokes books it for the elevator. Orr follows.

"Stay down here," she orders him. "Watch for anything."

Stokes reaches the thirteenth floor. The elevator doors open. Shotgun in hand, she peeks down the hallway. It's empty and still. The bodyguard's body lies limp and bloody on the carpet. She creeps along the wall toward the suite. She examines the body and notices the shattered skull. Brain matter on the wall. She doesn't bother checking a pulse.

The door is cracked. The latch has been shot out. She kicks it wide open and clears the corners. She scans the living room. "LAPD!" Nothing.

On the other side of the room, the bedroom door is also cracked. She makes her way over slowly, creeping soundless like a cat.

The teenage girl bursts through the door, making Stokes jump. The girl is naked and splattered with blood, her ankles still bound in rope.

"HELP ME!" she cries, hopping hysterically into Stokes's arms, bloodying up her clothes.

Stokes takes the bedding from off the floor and covers her up. "Where are you hurt?"

"It's—it's not my blood," the girl answers. "Three other girls came in. They cut me loose, but then they—" her eyes are wild with shock. "I don't know who they were. It happened so fast. It was so easy how they did it," she starts sobbing. "It's like they had claws. They just ripped his—"

Loud cackles echo from the bathroom. They both freeze.

"They can't still be in here," the girl panic-whispers. "They chased the other one out—"

Stokes racks the shotgun. CLICK-CLACK. She flips out her switchblade and cuts the girl's ankles loose. "Get downstairs to the lobby," she orders. "Tell them to call an ambulance."

The girl doesn't waste a second and disappears out the door and down the hallway, dragging the bedding with her.

"LAPD!" Stokes yells as she enters the bedroom

and moves on the bathroom. "Come out slowly with your hands up!"

As expected, there's no response. She takes one slow step after the other, the barrel of the shotgun leading the way. She's right outside the bathroom door—

From inside the bathroom, something heavy gets hurled at Stokes. It nails her right in the face, causing her to stumble and fall on her ass. The shotgun goes off. Chunks of ceiling fly everywhere. She touches her cheek. It's cold and wet. She looks at her hand. Blood. She looks on the floor where the thing that hit her landed. It's a severed head of one of the men. Its eyelids halfway closed, mouth agape, thinning hair caked in blood.

The cackling echoes again.

Stokes racks the shotgun and fires through the wall. She racks and fires again. More debris flies and gun smoke fills the room. Her ears ring. She racks again and jumps around the corner, firing blindly. The shower door shatters and explodes. The tile is pocked with pellets. She's stunned when she finds the bathroom empty. Nothing there but the slumped, headless corpse of the man in the blue polo.

She turns around, frantically searching the rest of the suite. There's nothing.

She hears commotion outside in the hotel's driveway. She peers out the window. Down below, the man in the red polo limps toward the Macan and hops in. It peels off.

Stokes cell phone rings. She answers. It's Orr.

"Get down here. A Porsche SUV just tore off and

I saw our ladies exit out the back. One of 'em was buck naked! They refused to stop when I ordered them. I think they're after that Porsche. Stokes, they…looked so—"

"Just have the car ready, Orr."

D_J Gidget speaks in a low and ominous tone—unable to totally drop her native surfer tongue—she does her best Orson Welles:

"We know now that in the early years of the twenty-first century, this world was being watched closely by intelligences greater than—whoa-man's. With infinite complacence people went to and fro over the earth about their little affairs, assured of their dominion over this small spinning ball of surf and turf, which by chance or design whoa-man has inherited out of the dark mystery of TimeSpace. Yet across an immense ethereal gulf, intellects vast, cool, and unsympathetic regarded this earth with envious eyes and slowly and surely drew their plans against us. In the twentieth year of the twenty-first century came the great disillusionment. The invasion has begun, fellow humans. Prepare for 'The Attack of the Giant Ants' by Blondie here on KXLA."

The opening drum roll begins. Sirens, gun fire, screams, and explosions light the street bright as the summer sun.

Still stark naked, the Passenger lights the wick of a pipe bomb and hurls it out of the Road Runner. Palm trees and upscale chains whir by in the background as it lands several feet from the Charger and explodes. Stokes and Orr feel the impact as the Charger is rocked and swerves into oncoming traffic.

"Jesus fuck!" Orr screams.

They lose ground on the Road Runner and fall behind dodging traffic. It's high-speed chaos as the Charger chases the Road Runner and the Road Runner chases the Macan.

Stokes recovers and gets on the right side of the road. She observes the trio in the flesh for the first time. Their visage stops the heart and cuts off the breath, the reality of encountering something masquerading as human. She notes their features. The one driving has red hair, the one throwing bombs has yellow hair, and the one in the backseat has shaved orange hair. She makes the connection that red and yellow make orange. What's the significance? No time to think, she's losing the Road Runner.

The Driver steps on the gas and gains on the Macan, smashing its rear bumper. She points the .45 out the window and opens fire. Bullets tear through the body of the Macan and back windows bust. The man in the red polo cries in fear. His chauffeur threads the needle through the intersection at Olympic, trying to lose the Road Runner but with no luck. The Driver follows with ease, driving with one hand and rapid-firing with the other.

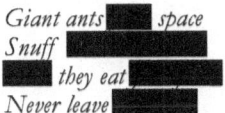

Giant ants ▮▮ *space*
Snuff ▮▮▮▮▮
▮▮ *they eat* ▮▮▮
Never leave ▮▮▮

Sheriff patrol comes outta nowhere in pursuit, getting in Stokes' way and making her lose sight of the Road Runner.

The Passenger looks back at their pursuers. She lights the fuse of another pipe bomb and chucks it.

An explosion rocks the undercarriage of a patrol car, sending it rolling on its side into the glass windows of an upscale store front.

"Fucking Barney blue Fife fucks," Stokes spits. She picks up the mic on the mobile. "In pursuit of the wanted, north on Beverly Drive. Be advised, suspects are armed with explosives. Stand the fuck down. I've got point."

Just as the other patrol cars fall behind, a dark blue sedan speeds ahead and cuts Stokes off. She gets around it and pulls up side by side. It's hard to see inside through the tinted windows.

"Who the hell's that?" Orr yells.

"I'm guessing our friends at the Bureau," Stokes says calmly. She jerks the wheel and slams into their driver side door. The feds lose control and veer into the sidewalk, crashing into a palm tree. Pedestrians fly every which way.

shoot fire
Tokyo burns
drowns
The moon

The Macan cuts a sharp right onto Santa Monica Boulevard, fishtailing wildly. The Driver hits the handbrake and sends the Road Runner into a controlled skid. She whips the wheel and accelerates and gains on the Macan. The Road Runner's guttural engine screams in high gear. Stokes takes the sharp turn, does the same trick with the handbrake, stays in control and guns it. The smell of burnt rubber. Loose car parts creak.

The Driver throws more lead at the Macan, emptying the magazine. Slugs cut through the body, more windows shatter as the man in the red polo covers his head under the seat. The chauffeur swerves around palm trees in the center divider, barely able to see with his head ducked down. They roar through the red light at Doheny Drive, oncoming traffic scatters and skids and crashes into each other. Like a race car driver at Daytona, Stokes finds the holes in the chaos of the intersection and steps on the gas.

The Passenger lights the fuse of another pipe bomb, lobs it out of the Road Runner. Then another, then another, then another.

Stokes avoids the explosions like a minefield. A few civilian cars catch the brunt and go up in a blaze. Curtains of fire materialize. Burning hands claw at the windows.

The Driver reloads the .45 and opens fire again. This time, her aim was true. She puts three bullets through the driver's seat of the Macan. The chauffeur's body slumps over the wheel and the Macan cuts sharply toward the sidewalk and collides with a parked car.

The Driver slams the breaks and pulls up behind the scene of twisted metal. She grabs rope from the backseat and tosses the .45 to the Passenger who turns around and immediately fires at Stokes and Orr as they approach.

Bullet holes litter the Charger's windshield. Stokes stops the car. She and Orr draw their pistols, open their respective doors, take cover, and fire back at the Road Runner.

Crowds scream and scatter. Patrol cars are still far behind. Chopper materializes overhead.

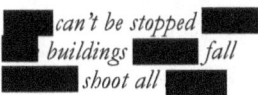

can't be stopped
buildings *fall*
shoot all

The Driver slithers low over to the Macan, avoiding whizzing slugs. She opens the door as the man in the red polo lets out a shriek. With one hand, she drags him out by his hair, and hogties him with freakish speed. She motions for the Backseat Third to come and help her. The Backseat Third shows reluctance. The Driver's shock is outweighed only by her anger. She motions again for her to come help, this time more adamantly. The Backseat Third refuses. Short on time, the Passenger helps instead, and they carry the tied hog and toss him into the back of the Road Runner as the Passenger continues firing at Stokes and Orr.

Shrapnel ricochets all over the Charger. Bullet holes pelt the doors and hood. Orr is hit twice in the chest.

They pile into the Road Runner and take off.

In shock, Orr falls back and sits in the passenger seat. Stokes hasn't even realized what's happened. She gets back in and steps on the gas.

They burn through the Norma Triangle in pursuit. Stokes and the Passenger exchange fire through the intersection of San Vincente Boulevard. The girls' red and yellow hair whip around in the wind, looking like flames.

The world is ███████
███████ *lost*
Mankind is ███████
███████ *void*
██ *la* ███████
La la la la la
███████ *la.*

Orr struggles to breathe. Stokes finally notices his

wheezing and turns to see his clothes soaked in blood, hands clutched against the wound. She puts down her pistol and picks up the mic, "We've got an officer wounded, still in pursuit of the suspects, east on Santa Monica approaching La Cienega." She hangs up. "Hold on, Larry, we'll get you right."

Stokes debates whether to keep on their tail, or to pull over and get Orr the help he needs. She resents having a choice. Just as she's about to decide, she sees something she doesn't believe. She squints her eyes, making sure she's not seeing things.

The Backseat Third is cutting the man in the red polo loose. She and the Passenger struggle before she wins out and tosses him from the car.

His body tumbles and rolls. Stokes swerves to avoid hitting him.

The Backseat Third then reaches over and grabs the wheel. All three struggle—punching, biting, scratching, gouging, pulling, yanking. The Driver loses control. The Road Runner veers into oncoming traffic right in front of the IHOP and smashes into an SUV. Several other cars follow and a massive pile-up ensues. Stokes speeds past the carnage and slams on the breaks, skidding it sideways, nearly hitting a crowd in the crosswalk. She turns to look. The Road Runner flips and tumbles and a large explosion splits the old whip in half. The blast ravages the cars around it and sets off a chain reaction. Sounds of exploding hell rumble through the West Hollywood corridor.

Everything's in post-blast shock. Stokes gets out of the car and rushes to the scene, desperate to get to the Road Runner. The heat's enough to melt flesh and a delayed explosion knocks her on her back. Next thing she knows, witnesses are dragging her away from the inferno and onto the sidewalk. She shakes away the daze and lumbers back to the Charger. Before she picks up the mic, she looks over to check on Orr. He's no longer breathing, eyes fixed and dilated.

———————

Cigarette smoke twirls around the dead-calm hand of Stokes. From the edge of Santa Monica Boulevard, she gazes down La Cienega's descent—neon signage sparks up in the early evening—observing the iconic NORMS sign and the Beverly Center and the carpet of lights beyond in the twinkling lowlands.

The beauty of the city seems cruel in its indifference to the horrid scene just a few hundred feet away. The entire block of Santa Monica Boulevard is shut down, painted by red and blue flashing lights that never stop, as first responders clean up the mess in worker bee fashion.

"No bodies were found in the wreckage," Captain Mannix reports. "Their little collection of pipe bombs must've gone off in the crash."

Stokes passively listens, zoned out, her ears still ringing. An EMT tends to her gashes and cuts and checks for a concussion.

"No bodies," Stokes echoes.

"No bodies," Mannix echoes back.

An aftershock rumbles through the city.

Stokes takes a deep inhale, the smoke pours out of her nostrils. "How do you suppose that's possible?"

Mannix shrugs, "You know these streets get a lot stranger than you do, Stokes. One time, long ago, when I was on beat, after a ten car pile-up on the 5, there were two bodies we couldn't account for. When the sun came up the next day, we realized both bodies had been ejected and launched clear onto the freeway sign above. They were just crumpled up there, already being pecked at by crows. I'll never forget the sight. Point is, you encounter some weird shit on the job. You know it as well as I do. But, however weird, no human could walk away from what happened today."

"I walked away, didn't I?"

"There's that wit. Look, you got your man, Detective. You always do. Take it easy, now."

Stokes isn't feeling witty, though. She's skeptical. She's more than skeptical. She's certain. She resents her own intuition, it's been right more times than she's wanted.

"Your men over at the Marriott?" Stokes asks, "What did they come back with?"

"The two men at the hotel were identified. The poor headless bastard is James E. Smith, Chairman and CEO of J.P. Morgan. The one they took for their little joyride is Hugh Friedberg, Vice President and CEO of Monsanto. He's at Cedar Sinai in critical condition."

"Do we have an I.D. on these hellcats yet? The hotel must have some camera footage."

"Same issue as the bank. The picture's distorted. Their faces and bodies come out like blurry heat signatures. It's damnedest thing."

"Goddamnit," Stokes breathes smoke.

Mannix hands her three dirty pipe bombs. "We

were able to recover a few of their toys. Big mothers. Whoever these punks were, they weren't fucking around."

"Or whatever they were…" Stokes says under her breath. She takes the pipe bombs from Mannix, feeling their weight.

"They had a nice little hit list."

"I guess that explains the feds," Stokes scoffs.

"That's another thing. I'm taking heat from the Bureau. We got two of their agents in critical condition."

"Bad things can happen in a car chase. Those Ivy League cops should be more careful."

"Mel, I asked for quiet and swift. Not for you to burn half of West Hollywood all to hell and leave a trail of dead in your wake. Now I gotta take it up the ass from WeHo officials. The sheriff, too."

"You wanted the desk job."

"Is that what this is about? I rise fast?"

Stokes looks at him like he's stupid. She lights another cigarette.

Mannix collects himself and cools off. "Too bad about Orr. Maybe he was out of his element. I should've kept this whole thing in-house."

"I could've told you that."

"Thanks for the support."

"You don't pay me for sympathy."

"No. We pay you to be invisible. Next time, do

your fucking job."

Stokes gets up, squashes her cigarette and walks away. "Then trust me when I say I don't want a fucking partner. Unless more dead is what you're after."

————

When Stokes gets to the West L.A. precinct, she's met more with silent and wary head nods than with applause. A high-profile collar with a high body count gets you notoriety at best.

There's a white, unmarked envelope waiting for her on her desk. She looks around. She asks the detective a few desks over who delivered it and he shrugs and says he doesn't know and that he didn't see anybody. She opens it with caution.

It's a simple piece of paper. She unfolds it, and letters are glued together from magazine cut-outs like in a ransom letter:

"I am 1 of 3… I cun no longer see… I dun noe hoo I bee… I furget wy by Mother I wus decreed… But all I wunna do is flee flee flee… Plz offiserrr ladee… My sissters will soon find me… Help me bee… Help me bee… Golden Star Motel #3."

It took a minute to decipher its meaning. What she knew for sure was who it was from. The one in the backseat of the Road Runner who untied the victim and tossed him from the car. The one with the shaved orange hair and orange lipstick and orange eyes. The one who had betrayed her so-called sisters.

They're still alive. She knew it, as disturbing as it was.

She knew the motel too. It's on Pico. It's a shit hole. She ran a few stings there. Drug deals. Solicitation. Child predation. Nothing ever went right at the Golden Star Motel. Maybe it's a trap.

Even more foreboding is the prose of the letter itself. It rattles the spine just to read something so playful yet so perturbing by a nonhuman intelligence. In her vision quest with Hector, it was revealed where they came from—below, within—but what is it that they want? Now Stokes is led to believe there's a schism between these three? And that this traitor is reaching out to her for help? How could she help? Keep this creature in protective custody? And what happens when they finally came for her? How can they be stopped? Endless questions stir in Stokes' rattled head. But one thing is certain, she's got an address, which is more than anything she's had in the last twenty four hours.

She hears some commotion on the other side of the room. A bunch of officers crowd the window, all looking at the same thing in the sky. Others have rushed outside into the parking lot to get a better look. She follows.

Three orbs of amber light hover in the distance over the Capital Records building.

"What the fuck are those?" an officer yells out.

"Earthquake lights," an old timer behind her says. "I've seen them before. Been years though."

"What do you mean? Earthquake lights?" Stokes asks.

"It's an unexplained phenomenon, but it happens. Look where they're at. Hovering directly over the Hollywood fault line. That fault line runs parallel between Hollywood Boulevard and Yucca, and cuts straight through Cahuenga, Vine, Argyle, and Gower. Man, L.A. is cracking in two."

The Santa Ana winds kick up. Strong gusts whip palm trees and electrical lines and create auditory hallucinations in the ears of Angelenos. The city is on edge.

Then the crowd of officers 'ooh' and 'ahh' when the lights begin moving. They dance around each other until one of them vanishes, leaving only two remaining. Just hovering there, two of them.

The words of the druggist echoes in her mind.

"Watch the lights," Stokes whispers.

She looks at the letter still in her hand. Maybe it's a trap. It probably is. But what choice did she have?

———————

Chery Glaser comes on the radio with local news, "A brushfire that started in Griffith Park just a few hours ago has now spread into residential areas. It does not bode well for firefighting efforts or for Hollywood residents as Southern California is battered with winds exceeding forty miles per hour. Stay with us for updates into the night—"

Stokes twists the dial. She only needs one guess as to who started the fire. Through the static—

"This is DJ Gidget with more dirty ditties for you on Garage Rock Jams here on KXLA. Hollywood is burning, haven't you heard? It was only a matter of time, but, hey, you can't kill us that easy. Here's 'Hard To Kill' by Bleached."

The dark and empty Woodlawn Cemetery passes on the right. Winds rush through its tombstones like restless ghosts.

A man photographs a woman in high heels and short skirt in front of the old art deco façade of the Golden Star Motel as Stokes pulls into the small parking lot. You couldn't stage this kind of sleaze if you tried.

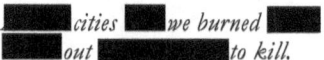

Stokes rolls slowly past the front office, illuminated by the vacancy sign glowing red. The desk clerk is on the nod, slumped back in his chair, head hung low, and behind him a white board with signs reading NO GUNS and NO DRUGS and NO MUSIC. There also hangs a NO PETS sign with the word PETS scratched out and ANIMALS written in its place. NO ANIMALS. The old TV is going with bad static and images of the growing Hollywood fire.

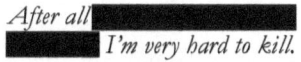

After all ▮▮▮▮▮▮▮▮▮▮▮
▮▮▮▮▮ *I'm very hard to kill.*

Stokes parks and approaches room number three, gun out.

No lights on inside.

She kicks the door in. It cracks but the deadlatch catches. She kicks again, harder. The door busts open. It's the smell that hits her first. Musty. Murky. She feels around the walls for a light switch, scanning the blackness in front of her, barrel first. She hits the light, illuminating the room's 70's-era fake wood paneling and dirty carpet stained in browns and yellows.

Scrawled all over the walls in fresh blood:

TrHateHer TrHateHer TraitHerTrait HerTraitHer TraitHer

TrHateHer TrHateHer TraitHerTrait HerTraitHer TraitHer

TrHateHer TrHateHer TraitHerTrait HerTraitHer TraitHer

TrHateHer TrHateHer TraitHerTrait HerTraitHer TraitHer

TrHateHer TrHateHer TraitHerTrait HerTraitHer TraitHer

TrHateHer TrHateHer TraitHerTrait HerTraitHer
TraitHer

On the floor is a patch of blood—streaked as if a body had been dragged through it. She follows the trail, snaking into the bathroom.

She hits the light and freezes. Behind the translucent shower curtain is a dark figure.

"Out of the shower, now! Hands on your head. Intertwine your fingers. No sudden moves, or I'm putting two through your fucking eyes."

The figure doesn't move. No sounds other than slow water drips from the faucet.

Stokes approaches the shower. She tears open the curtain.

The Backseat Third is dead, hanging naked and limp, hands tied around the shower head. Her fingers have been cut off. Her eyes and tongue have been cut out. Mouth agape. Blood and water pools around the clogged drain.

Stokes whips around, expecting the other two to be behind her. The motel room is empty.

The world is vacuum. There's no noise, even in the silence.

She turns back to the body. So, these things can die. She notices something strange. Upon closer inspection, there are fresh burn marks, like streaks, running down head to toe. She watches as a drop of yellow water builds on the shower faucet just above her head. It finally falls, hitting the forehead, burning the skin like sulfuric acid. Were they torturing her—with water?

She looks down and notices something clogging the drain. She reaches and pulls it out. Big gargle noise as the bloody water all goes down. It's a wadded-up piece of stationary paper. She opens it. There's writing scrawled in runny black ink:

U CUNT STOP US

HA

HA

HA

She drops the paper and watches it flutter back to the bottom of the tub. The swirl of red circling the drain puts her into trance. Her legs wobble. Everything goes black.

Stokes awakens on the bathroom floor to a primal scream. She jolts, grabs her gun. Nothing. Did she hear that, or was it in her head? She looks to the corpse and it's still staring at her with two hollow eyes.

There's a vision in her mind. Somewhere she needs to go. Clear as that scream. A scene. A place. And the urgency to head straight into it at full speed.

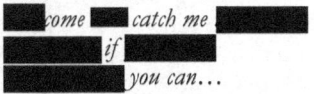

come *catch me*
if
you can...

But first, there's something she feels she must do, and she doesn't know why, but this is no time for knowledge. Just pure, unrelenting instinct.

———————

"This is DJ Gidget bringing you the heat as the city burns. They've issued evacuation orders for everyone everywhere. But if they think we're giving up rock 'n' roll for staying alive, they've got another thing coming. Here's The Runaways with 'I Love Playin' With Fire.' Don't touch that dial, we're gonna keep the wax spinning until it melts here on KXLA."

Deep in Topanga Canyon, Stokes imagines Hector performing some rain dance—a water prayer.

From Coliseum Street, she turns the bullet hole-ridden Charger onto the 3800 block of South Norton Avenue. The street's idyllic, suburban sprawl makes her, for an instant, forget the inferno just a few miles north eating Hollywood. Its distant flames fill her rearview mirror.

She parks and gets out. Nothing on the dark street except for gusts of wind that knock over garbage cans. She walks up to Larry Orr's house and knocks on the front door. His widow answers. A startling, pale face with red eyes.

"I already got the phone call. Thanks."

Just as the widow closes the door, Stokes stops it with her foot, "We worked together. On this last case..."

Inside, the 1950 ranch-style home smells the way

Orr smelled. She never noticed his scent until now. Firefighter figurines and novelty toys litter the mantle and table tops. Framed above the brick fireplace is Orr's firefighter uniform. On the opposite wall hangs a framed poster of the 1975 film *The Day of the Locust.*

"This world is taking everything from me," the widow tells her. "I was frantically trying to reach him last night. But his phone kept going to voicemail. I guess there wasn't service where he was."

"Yeah, we, uh—" Stokes hesitates to speak further, "we were in a patchy area."

"But now, I'm glad he was spared…"

There's an unnerving calm in her voice. The widow drifts down the hallway and into a bedroom.

Confused, Stokes follows.

It's a nursery. The decorating remains unfinished. The reddened sky outside glows through the lace curtains.

The widow looks down into an empty crib, "He didn't make it through the night."

Stokes says nothing, just hangs her head in respect.

"And then, just today, I got the call about Larry. It didn't seem real. Nothing seems real anymore. What's been happening. Earthquakes. Fires. Terror. It all seems surreal, alien, until it happens to you."

Stokes reaches for platitudes. She doesn't want to confirm this poor woman's existential dread, "Orr… Larry…was a good man. I was lucky to have him by my side—"

"There are things you're supposed to do to protect

a child in its crib," the widow continues. "Old Jewish superstitions. Are you familiar with the story of Lilith, Detective? Adam's first wife?"

"I am."

"You're supposed to keep amulets around. Amulets of the three angels God sent to try to bring Lilith back to the Garden of Eden. But she refused, vowing to take the sons of mankind. The amulets are spiritual protection. I'm not a superstitious person. I was never religious. I never listened to my mother. I didn't want to put that on my boy. Now she blames me. She says that something evil took my son, that I didn't protect him."

There's a moment of silence. The widow looks at Stokes, "My friends are worried about me. They think I've lost it. But you don't seem shocked."

"I'm not."

Stokes knew it would come to this. But it's pure hubris to think there was anything to be done about it. Just like an earthquake. Just like a firestorm. Just like three hellcats rising up out of this ancient dirt to lay waste to man's land. Things just happen.

There wasn't any justice for something like this. Nobody comes back from it. And if you ever hope to move forward, you get raked through the coals. There wasn't any justice. Not ever. And the longer she stays in this job, the more abstract that word becomes. But Stokes wasn't in it for justice. That was her old partner. She was the one who believed in absolutes like justice. That it was blind. That it could be dispensed. Stokes never knew the things her partner knew. She just knew L.A.—an illusion—an aberration—where nothing is absolute—and to act accordingly. And she knew "her man" was still out there. Human or not.

Hell has come a-knockin', and she intends to be the one to answer the door. But there's no reason this widow should endure any more.

"Look, the firestorm is headed this way," Stokes tells her. "It's eating everything. They've ordered a city-wide evacuation—"

"It's not for me. I've lived in this city all my life. I have nothing left to take. I'm ready for it to burn," the widow smiles warmly, and, for a moment, the guilt that drove Stokes here is assuaged. Beyond the bottomless pit into which the city is being pulled, maybe there's light, as invisible as it seems. But forward first—through the fire.

"Would you like some black coffee?" the widow asks. "Sorry, but I'm out of cream." The widow leaves the room. Off in the kitchen, she's heard heating up the kettle.

Stokes walks out into the hallway, and is drawn to the master bedroom. She goes to the walk-in closet, turns on the light. Her eyes light up at what she sees inside, hanging at the far end. Below that is a footlocker. She kneels down and opens it. Her face splits into an awful smile, "Orr, you devil...."

———————

The precinct is near-deserted. Stokes walks into the parking structure, looking over her shoulder, trying not to look suspicious. She's not authorized to be here. The few officers around wouldn't question her actions anyway, likely because of the current state of chaos, and likely because of what she's wearing. Nobody would dare question anything she's doing.

She climbs into a Lenco BearCat, one of those big, armored beasts used by SWAT. She's still got the three pipe bombs that were recovered earlier that day, now all duct-taped together and their fuses twisted into one.

She puts the key in the ignition and drops it into reverse, peeling out onto the street. It's got a lot more kick than she thought for such a heavy bastard.

The BearCat screams into the firestorm like a bat into hell on Santa Monica Boulevard. Flames materialize along the sidewalk as the buildings and cars and palm trees burn. The corridors are abandoned. The dry L.A. earth is coming apart, everything is moving and shifting, roads are disintegrating, landmarks collapse into caverns below.

Any living thing caught on the street is scorched to a pillar of salt.

Stokes pushes further into the heat, passing Doheny Drive and engulfed relics like Dan Tana's Restaurant and the Troubadour. She's heading straight into that vision she had in the motel room—the place, the intersection. She turns left on La Cienega, climbing the steep hill toward Sunset Boulevard. Flaming debris and ash fall on the BearCat and all around her.

She turns right on Sunset, swerving around abandoned cars, passing The Comedy Store, The Standard Hotel, billboards overhead advertising a bygone world, passing The Body Shop—scorched icons all—pedal to the floor. The RPM's rev into the red.

She sees it, her vision, up ahead, at the boulevard bend. The entrance to the Châteaux Marmont at Sunset and Marmont Lane. She's not slowing down and doesn't know why. She prepares for the impact.

Just as she's about crash into the hotel, a black flash passes in front of her. BAM. She hits the rear end of a speeding car, changing her trajectory and skidding the BearCat around onto the curb. The black car she hit spins in chaos a few times on Sunset before screeching to a stop.

———————

Shaking off the daze, Stokes looks to see who it is. Staring back at her through the windshield are the Driver and the Passenger.

They're just as surprised as Stokes. It seems she's interrupted their fuel-injected traipse through a burning Hollywood inferno.

They're both naked. Their hair flows like lava. Their eyes are total black. They see what Stokes is wearing, what she took from his closet—Larry Orr's old silvers—a fire proximity suit complete with aluminized jacket and pants with neck shroud and hood. Their smiles grow from ear to ear. Stokes has come to play.

"Sunset Strip R.I.P." starts playing on the radio. "The studio's on fire now," announces DJ Gidget. "I'm not sure how much longer we'll last. Enjoy this hot track by The Flytraps while you still can. We sure will. Cling to your loved ones and feel the burn with us here on KXLA—"

They drive a black 1969 Dodge Charger RT Hellcat, as if to mimic Stokes—to mock her. She'll give them something to mock.

"Joyride's over, ladies."

She steps out of the BearCat. She takes out the IFEX 3000 that she found in Orr's closet along with the suit. It's an impulse firefighting gun capable of shooting high-velocity bursts of water—a backpack of two tanks and a hose connected to what looks like a shotgun.

She approaches the Charger like it's a routine traffic stop. She releases the water valve on the gun like cocking a hammer. She points the barrel at the Passenger's head. Their devilish smiles fade. She pulls the trigger. The blasts shatters the window and hits the Passenger point blank in the head. Half of the skin and hair on her head burns away. The Passenger shrieks in agony. Water vapor fills the inside of the car and burns the Driver too. She drops the shifter and takes off. Tires spin and smoke as they speed away.

Stokes takes out her Smith & Wesson and opens fire, trying to take out their tires. Bullets rain on the Charger.

rock and roll
reign
beauty fade
rotting *grave.*

Stokes hurries back to the BearCat and gets in. The chase ensues.

The Charger makes a hard left up Laurel Canyon and into the winding hills.

Ash covers the street like dirty snow and everything is lit in blinding gold.

Stokes keeps them in sight and catches up as they reach Mount Olympus. Armed with a custom AKMS with shortened barrel, the Passenger—half face/half skull—hangs out the window and fires back with a barrage of bullets. The spray pelts the steel and ricochets off the BearCat's windshield. Stokes rams the rear of the Charger, the Passenger struggles to hold on. She grits her teeth and continues firing. The Laurel Canyon Country Store passes on the right as it smolders.

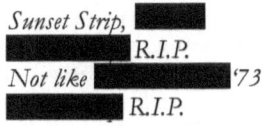

Stokes pulls up on their left and smashes into the driver side door. Still hanging out the window, the Passenger fires over the roof. The canyon echoes with pops of the machine gun. Both cars skid and veer into the rough, unpaved shoulder, kicking up dirt. The street zig-zags and Stokes loses ground on the Charger.

She watches the Passenger duck back into the car, and manually empty the machine gun's magazine. She reloads it with different bullets. The Passenger wastes no time and fires out of the back window of the Charger as the glass shatters. A few of the slugs penetrate the BearCat and Stokes hears them ping around inside.

She feels a rush of panic. "Shit."

The street straightens out briefly before it reaches Mulholland Drive. Stokes pulls up to their left again, determined to take them out for good. The vehicles collide with the sound of grinding metal. Stokes is about to wreck them into the jagged hillside. The Passenger hangs out the window—inches away from the rocks zipping by—and fires over the roof. This time, the bullets pierce the BearCat and one hits Stokes in the hip. She takes her foot off the gas and the Charger gets loose and speeds ahead. The Driver takes a right on Mulholland Drive.

Stokes checks her wound. She covers it with duct tape and wraps the roll around her thigh and waist, creating pressure. Bites off the excess and pulls tighter. She screams.

Stokes drops into low gear and follows them. There's a sharp sting now using the gas pedal. She winces trying to keep up around the sharp turns as the chase ensues through the Mulholland corridor. And now Stokes has to duck as armor-piercing bullets shoot through the windshield. Fire crews duck and dodge the gunfire while they save the mansions on stilts along the peaks of the Santa Monica Mountains. The canyon echoes with pops of the machine gun. Stokes follows the muzzle flash and gains speed. Bullets snap at the hood. Won't be long 'til they fuck the engine up and she'll be a sitting duck.

She loses the Charger around a turn and when she clears it, the taillights have vanished. The Charger disappeared.

———————

The BearCat slows down and Stokes scans the road. When she checks her side view mirrors, headlights flash on behind her. The Charger comes roaring with a hail of bullets. Stokes leans over the steering wheel, ducking bullets, and floors it.

The Passenger chucks pipe bombs and the blasts rock the BearCat back and forth. They're trying to flip the fucker. The half-face/half-skull Passenger is more than frustrated by how much Stokes isn't dying.

The Cahuenga Pass approaches. Stokes cuts right. A pipe bomb misses and takes out the light at Mulholland and Barham. She crosses the overpass above a desolate 101 Freeway. Then left. Then right again, making them work for their target. She sees signs for the Hollywood Reservoir, decides to crash through the north gate and down the private road that snakes the edge of the lake. She watches as a heli-tanker hovers down low to draw water out of the lake and then flies away.

The Driver and Passenger aren't fazed, they're not letting up. The BearCat is more holes than metal now. The AKMS cuts through it like hot butter. The narrow, winding road slows Stokes down and the Charger catches up beside her—naked wraiths staring straight at her. The Passenger has just reloaded and takes aim. Stokes doesn't hesitate and fires another high-velocity water round into the Charger. They lick their wounds and the Charger falls behind.

Stokes guns it onto the old Art Deco road of the Mulholland Dam. Over the railing, to her right, is the steep drop-off of the dam's concrete face—a dense hillside that rolls down into endless abyss. To her left, Lake Hollywood reflects the surrounding fire. It's placid and beautiful compared to the hell around it. The Hollywood Sign, in the distance above, is being eaten by monster flames.

The Driver screams pedal-to-the-floor and rides up on the right side of the BearCat this time. The Passenger hangs out the window, firing wildly. Stokes ducks below the dash, driving blind. She's not going to last much longer. It's only a matter of time. They may take this city but not before she takes them first. She grabs the three pipe bombs, and lights the fuse.

The Passenger's body vibrates with gunfire. It's an awesome sight—silhouette of the Charger and her hair whipping on her half-skull and the gun blasting as the inferno blankets the mountains beyond.

The Charger pulls up out in front of the BearCat. The Passenger stops firing. Stokes sits up to face them. The Passenger has a clear shot. She smiles that alien smile, ear to ear, and takes aim.

An earthquake hits. Much stronger than yesterday. Both vehicles are jerked violently to the right and crash through the railing. They roll over the edge and land on the hillside below.

The quake rips a huge crack in the dam. The water is rough now, choppy surf banging against the curved walls. The pressure's building. It's all being held together by a thread now.

The earth stops. Stokes comes to. She feels the pull of the steep hill. She's in ubiquitous pain. She's in the dirt. She's not in the BearCat. She looks around, orients herself. The BearCat is about a hundred feet away, upside down, up against the base of the dam. The fresh crack runs vertically up the length of the wall. The dam moans.

The red taillights of the Charger shine through the brush. It's not far and landed on its wheels. Stokes can see their bare legs through the undercarriage of the car as they both step out. They lurch toward her, bloody and painful.

She remembers she lit the fuse. She checks around to see if it's anywhere near. She doesn't see it. It must still be in the BearCat.

One…two…three.

They reach Stokes and loom over her. She's vulnerable, wounded, easy prey now. The Driver and Passenger look down at her, their skulls exposed through dripping, melted flesh, "Water—hurts," the Driver taunts. "But—it—won't—save—you."

"A little fire might."

BOOM.

The blast of the mega pipe bomb splits the crack in the dam apart. The Driver and Passenger look on in horror at the dark rift, howling in release, as a deluge of water fills the ravine. Even Stokes is shocked how quickly it comes on. She doesn't get the chance to see the water rip their flesh from the bone and all get wiped away down into the endless abyss. The flood pins her against a tree and she holds on with all she's got left.

It's hard to say how much time passes before a buzzing is heard and a spotlight shines from above. A rescue worker dangles from a rope and grabs Stokes. "We're getting you outta here, Detective." They reel her into the chopper.

She's just one of many flashing lights in the sky now, flying on high over the precious acropolis of L.A.'s mountains and canyons.

No flashing lights are down below in the basin. If it weren't for Stokes getting her man like she always does, they probably just would've let it all burn. Exhausted and hurting, she watches as the Hollywood Reservoir empties its two and a half billion gallons of water down into the burning lowlands, making a murky river out of the 101. The flames are quelled and the city lies in a blanket of dying ember. The meek and meager and widowed are ash. But these hills will remain, and its grand estates impervious to catastrophe.

Even with the fires, the quakes, the floods, and Earth itself opening its mouth to swallow it whole, this city mutates and endures. The past always burns, but L.A. is a desert mirage, and its form always takes shape on the future horizon just out of reach.

Unfettered development will prop this movie set reality of a city back up again, and the illusion will go on. Whatever these women, these creatures, these harbingers of vengeance set out to achieve will be a mere blot on the storied apocalyptic paradise of Hollywood.

Stokes gazes out into the infinitude of it all, silent in her hollow victory.

Her eyes morph into total black.

Out Soon On Far West

farwestpress.com